FRAME OF IMAGINATION

COLLECTION OF SHORT STORIES

KALYAN KUMAR

Contents

Author

Part 2

1. The Sadness In The Anger — 5
2. A Sit-down Comeda — 10
3. A Melting Pops — 15
4. All Because Of A Tree — 17
5. Laughing At The Face Of Death — 21
6. Love And Hate — 24
7. Sleepless Nights — 28
8. Guess We All Know — 32
9. As If — 35
10. In The Cage — 37

Author

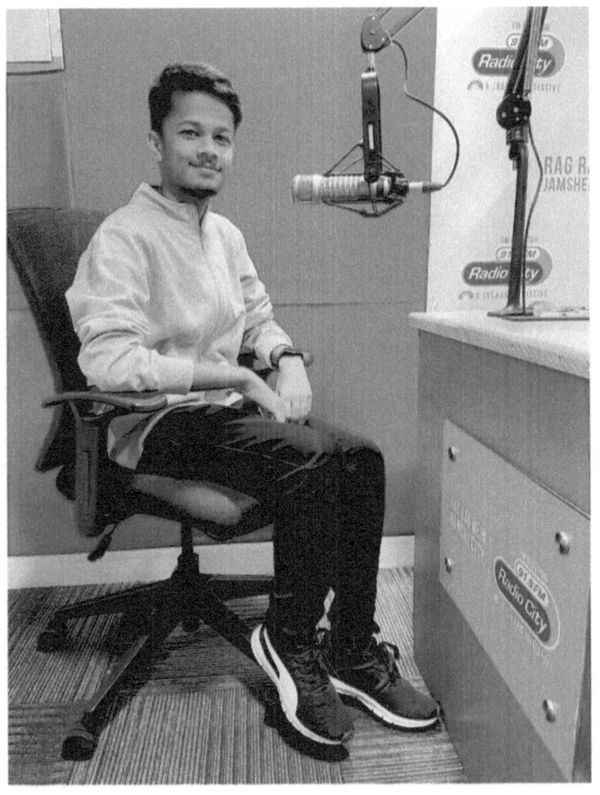

Mr. Kalyan Kumar (MCS Best Author of Year 2022)

A BOY WHO WAS LOST IN THE CROWD OF THIS WORLD
AND WAS AIMLESS

WAS LUCKY ENOUGH TO FIND HIS HOME IN A PERSON
WHO TOTALLY CHANGED HER FORTUNE!

CHAPTER ONE

The Sadness In The Anger

The loudest thing I have heard in my life is the silence between me and my wife when she concluded that she would be leaving me soon.

"I'm leaving," she says. "I'm going far, far away from you and Raivo. I want to."

It has only been an hour since she has moved in with me, so her luggage is still packed, standing behind the bedroom door.

We stare at each other, her eyes showing betrayal and rage, and mine showing surprise and distress, for a long time.

Finally, she walks back to her baggage, grasps them, and goes away, out the door, without looking back. It feels like my voice has abandoned me.

I sigh and look at the engagement ring I am wearing.

No. I have to keep my temper, and be mature. What would Raivo do if I, his dad, would get out of control?

I slowly but firmly take the ring out of my finger and glare at it. Without thinking twice, I throw the thing across the room.

"I hate you," I murmur. "I hate you... so much. But I also love you..." I shake my head swiftly. What the hell am I saying? I love her, but I hate her?

I hear a knock-knock on the main door. I immediately go to open it, blinking back my tears.

Startling enough, my sixteen-year-old son Raivo, who's in high school, appears and gives me a bear hug. "Dad! You told me Mom would be here when I come back. Where is she?"

I keep him in the embrace tightly. "Raivo, what... what if I tell you that we both have to live together alone... for now?"

Raivo pulls away from the hug. His expression shows confusion. "What? Is mom not back?"

"She..." I don't know how to tell him. This will definitely break him. And I don't to break him. But I have to... If I don't, he'll find out the hard way. And I guess he's old enough to handle this, right?

Raivo shouts, "Mom! Are you here?!"

No answer comes from anywhere, other than the wind rustling out the open door.

"Raivo, she left." I know this reply is too straight-forward, but he should know. He turns to face me. I continue, "She came here a while ago with her stuff, but left after saying she wants to be away from us."

He scowls. "No, she'd never," he says curtly. "She's not like that. You're joking. She's probs in the bathroom."

I knit my eyebrows. "She did leave."

Tears start welling up in Raivo's eyes. I can almost see his tough eyes turn to an ocean of tears. He purses his lips.

"I'm going to find her." He swings down his bagpack on the table and rushes down the corridor.

I clench my fists, knowing the attempt will be futile.

He comes back so fast I doubt he even reached the bedroom door. "She—maybe she isn't here yet."

As a dad with sixteen years of experience, I can sense the anger and contradictory denial in him.

I take a step closer to him. "She's gone," I whisper flatly, trying to not seem sad, even though my voice shakes. "She won't be back. She said she wants to be far, far away from us."

I feel the signs that his anger is about to go off the roof—his eyes going small, his brow tightened and, of course, his eyes getting watery.

Finally, tears come flowing. Thick, painful, grieving tears.

I go to try to take his hand, but he snatches it away.

"It's all your fault!" he shouts at me. He takes his bag and throws it to the floor. He kicks it away.

He walks back a few steps, still facing me and whimpering.

"She was a better parent than you! She was my mom! She was the best! It's your fault!"

His sad yet furious scowl makes me feel guilty. Why hadn't I tried to save this innocent boy? Why had I stayed voiceless when she was taking the last steps she'd take in this house? Why had I... I can't seem to admit it, but it's true...

Why had I been so in love with her?

Even though it's obvious, I can't let that sink in. She was obviously not in love with me like I was with her at all. Maybe this entire marriage was my fault.

My son's remark reverbates in my mind. It's all your fault!

As if on cue, he says it again. "Your fault entirely! You obviously didn't love me as your son! Mom wouldn't have left if you had asked her to stay!" He's now shouting a bit too loud now, his cheeks bright red.

"Raivo... Let me explain."

Raivo sits down on a chair. "You're just gonna make up some lame excuse! You-you are..." His voice quivers nervously. "You... you are the-the..."

A shiver goes down my spine when I realise he doesn't mean whatever he's going to say.

With a lot of stammering, he finally speaks up, "You are the worst f-father ever."

I take some steps towards him. His left hand is clenched tightly in a fist. He puts it on the table and unclenches.

I gasp quietly. "Raivo!" I whisper-yell.

In his fist is the engagement ring of his parents—me and his mom.

"Why'd you throw it on your room floor?!" Raivo exclaims, the hot ire surprisingly still in his voice.

"I was just..." I reach to take the ring.

But why do you want that ring? The rational side of my mind asks. It's not like you still love her, do you?

Crap. It's a rhetorical question.

Obviously you do, says my wife's voice in my head.

I say out loud, "Shut up."

"Answer me!" argues Raivo. "Why'd she ever leave her family?! ANSWER ME!"

That's it. Time to spill the truth.

I grab the ring from his hand. "She—your mom—didn't love us in the first place. She just—she felt sorry for me, and that's why she stayed with me all this time. She-she showed her true colors b-before leaving... forever."

Oh. Oh no. My voice is shaking. Why can't I speak properly?

My rational side argues, You are still in love with her. Just be grateful for having your son other than grieving some narcissist.

I hold on to the engagement ring. At least I can keep this... right? She'd have her ring so... we're stil technically together because there was no divorce? Wow, my desperation is terribly pathetic.

"Are you serious?" Raivo is a little calmer. "Do you know what she did for me?!"

I have a chance to win this argument now. "What'd she do for you, exactly?"

"She—" He leaves his mouth open. He can't find anything she did for him. "She, um, she talked to me!"

I raise my eyebrow, knowing it's a lie. "I also do."

"She..."

I put my hand on his shoulder. "Raivo, she did nothing. You just knew she and I were dating, so you considered her to be your mother. In fact, she did nothing to be even called a mother."

He closes his eyes, and he's crying angrily again. But this time it's for another reason. He isn't angry at me. He's angry at himself for forgetting that his so-called mother didn't do anything in his life. "You're right. I should've just listened to you... Dad."

He stands up and gives me slow hug again. It isn't full of excitement anymore... it's for comfort.

I hug him back tightly. "It's okay, Raivo. I'm sorry."

"Sorry? I'm the who should be sorry." He sniffles on my t-shirt. "Sorry, Dad. You're—"

I cut him off, "The worst father ever?" He gives a quiet regretful whimper.

"No, it's okay. I should've been better as a single parent. From this time on, I'll try to be the best father... ever."

CHAPTER TWO

A Sit-Down Comeda

"Everybody is a genius. But, if you judge a fish by its ability to climb a tree, it will spend its whole life believing that it is stupid."

~ ~ ~

There were two things I excelled at since I started breathing: Parkour and making jokes.

Sure, my studies were also... decent, I'd say, but humor and parkour were the things I geniunely enjoyed spending a long time on.

My school arranged an obstacle course for our physical education classes, and I was always the first.

My school was a different one, since it also had the subject of "Philosophy". And, yes, they taught it to kids starting from grade 2 to 12. The school also had a branched university, and that university also taught Philisophy.

It wasn't such a deep class—understanding the concept of life or the soul type of crap.

It was a much more interesting one. We were taught how to accept others' mentalities, understanding things from others' perspectives, about other people's feelings of helplessness, their firm beliefs, about the many religions, their motivations, and why some people's minds are the way they are. The classes were loved by all the students. By all, I mean ALL.

Even the students who were failing everything loved the Philosophy classes.

There was another thing I adored about the subject. A particular theme of the subject was also, coincidentally, humor.

We were taught to respect other people's sense of humor. We understood how other people wouldn't show their amusements by just laughing. Some people would grin, some would giggle, and some would make some bodily gesture. We were taught "dark humor" from grade 7. We were also taught about how people would lose their sense of humor as they get older and get more serious.

It helped me understand why I wouldn't laugh at my baby cousin's "fart" jokes, and why I didn't get the "coffin and coughing" jokes made by my dad.

Anyway, back to point: As much as I liked our Philosophy classes, it never overtook my love for Parkour. There was something special about placing your body parts on a specific place, jumping at a decided time, gaining momentum and bouncing off a trampoline. It was an exhilarating activity.

Only if someone had told me about the saying "Don't tempt fate."

As I was destined to be trapped in a wheelchair. Forever. Parkour was not for me.

It happened one winter when I went to slide sledges in the snow near the hills. My friends were with me.

They pushed me to slide down the icy hill. My sledge speeded down. And it hit a boulder. The rest is history.

The first time I went to school with my wheelchair, I actually cried seeing the other kids participate in the obstacle course. It was unfair. I actually considered getting off of my wheelchair, until I looked down to realise my feet were tied with a cotton cloth.

"Uhh..." I groaned, frustrated. I mean, I should've expected it though. The precise moment I wheeled my way in my house, I had tried to stand up. I had been a fool to do such a thing. Still I was stubborn. So my parents had no choice but to tie my feet together.

I sighed, and watched the kids bounce on trampolines wistfully.

Sadly, I could never do that again in my life again. Never. My doctors had said something about nerves twisting permanently, and that I couldn't run now. I didn't understand, probably because I was too busy mourning the death of my love for Parkour.

People judged me bitterly as I got older. They suggested that I tried to even just slowly walk. I knew I couldn't. I'd try to laugh it off with a joke suitable for every type of sense of humor, or make a really bad dad joke (hey, at least I still had my amazing humor and funniness!).

But they insisted. My brain developed as I matured, but it didn't stop from sometimes being a numbskull. Usually, being a numbskull is silly, fun, and mostly harmless.

But this one time it was the opposite of harmless.

On this particular day, as me and my friends chilled at his uncle's barnyard, he jokingly teased me, "Why don't you at least attempt to walk?"

And that was enough for me.

I replied, "Who said I didn't?" I lied, because I didn't want to get looked upon on anymore. But I took the lie incredibly, unbelievably far. "And I can walk. It just takes much more time."

"Then do it."

After that, my memory is blurry and hazy. I had stood up, somehow. And I had passed out right away, hearing some shouts and shrieks in my friend's voice. I remember feeling an indescribable type of pain in my left thigh. It felt like I should have been deleted out of existence. That's how it felt.

After that, I got to know I had gotten something called a "muscle spasm". I have no idea what that is, but it's hurtful.

The chances of me being able to walk decreased even more. It was horrible.

But something stayed with me. My humor. I realised that I could make a joke about almost anything in any situation. Thanksgiving, Christmas, a regular Sunday, about pancakes, and even a funeral. I had the jokes for all circumstances.

Something clicked in my mind when my older sister, Amy, suggested that I became a stand-up comedian. And she instantly regretted it, because it was ironic. Me, a person confined in a wheelchair, a STAND-UP comedian? Sounds like a joke I'd make in a hospital.

But it gave me an idea. Probably the most creative idea I've ever had.

I contacted my dad and asked him if he was going anywhere for a meet-up or something. He was a musician. He played the violin and guitar, and he often went on tours to perform.

He said yes, and that he was going to perform the next week in a nearby city. He was the first person I told about my idea. At first he laughed. He then told me it was great.

Two days before the flight, after we had packed, I told my friends and family about it. Naturally, they disagreed, argued, and tried to discourage me. They said that I was only good at Parkour, which I was incapable of now. I remember being furious at them and shutting myself in my bedroom.

Then my mother had asked from the keyhole, "Dear, I can tell you something. You shouldn't go on this trip. You are too weak, and you won't be able to do it. See, I have an idea. How about we give you prosthetics?"

I shouted, "No!" Prosthetics scare the hell out of me. They would make me feel inhumane, and robotic. And I had to always put them in, put them out. A big no for me.

After a few exchanges, mom finally walked away, angry with me. She still seemed to think I could do nothing but Parkour.

Fast forward two days later, after my dad and the others had performed, I was called to stage. I was a little nervous, granted.

But when the first questions was asked, everything was heavenly. Someone asked me if I was my dad's son. I replied, "Yeah, no! I'm my mom's son, duh!" The laugh that echoed through the room at my answer was enough to get me boosted.

The board above me read: MEET WEYLIN: THE SIT-DOWN COMEDIAN!

I made the entire crowd laugh. And yes, I remembered to keep my sense of humor inclusive and suitable for everyone. At least something I learned in school came in use.

After the show ended, I asked the crowd, "Would you guys come to a show of mine if I arrange another? One that is about joking about any subject of your choice?"

The crowd howled back in the affirmative.

"Great!" I said. "You'll choose what the subject will be! We'll give you some options on my dad's website!"

They roared excitedly yet again.

The show was an awesome experience. It made me get even more ideas for some dad jokes. I saved them up in a Google doc for another use.

One thing I've understood after years of my career in comedy—that you should never judge someone by an ability they are incapable of. Like I was.

They wouldn't understand that I was a funny person, and that I had potential in the career of humor. Still they insisted on me that only Parkour was for me.

I've lost count of how many places I've been to for my shows. Alas, I probably even visited Mars to a tour for aliens and forgot. I'm known by the name of Weylin, the sit-down comedian.

My craze of Parkour is long-gone now, and the only thing I'm worried about these days is whether I have enough ideas for yet another show

CHAPTER THREE

A Melting Pops

"Ugh! Not again!" Lily said in frustration after her Popsicle melted again for the 8th time that day.

"I'm just gonna go in a shade and try again, I guess," She said before buying another Popsicle and running to the nearest shade. She saw a tree and ran below it.

The Popsicle melted, yet again.

"I swear to God! If this happens again, I'm not even gonna try anymore. I already spent all of my pocket money on this!" She said. She got an idea and she brought an umbrella from her home.

"How can a Popsicle melt if there's no sunlight to begin with. Now, I will take it home and eat it happily," She said, walking to the store again.

"Can I get a medium Popsicle?" She asked.

"This is probably your tenth time asking me for a Popsicle. Why are you eating so many Popsicles? You will catch a cold," The store owner said before grabbing a Popsicle from the Refrigerator and handing it to Lily.

"That will be 75 cents," He said.

"What? You sold it for 50 cents all of the other times!" Lily said.

"I raised the price because I want full results of my hard work of dealing with you all day. You were my only customer for today," He said, frustrated.

"If I'm your only customer, then you should give me a discount and not raise the price!"

"You want the Popsicle or not?"

Lily let out a frustrated sigh and payed the full price.

After she payed, she was holding the Popsicle tightly.

She was very careful to defend the Popsicle from the sunlight, that she even forgot to put the umbrella over her head.

She slowly walked stop her house, and when she was below the roof's shade, she put the umbrella down and went to bite the Popsicle.

And before she knew it, the Popsicle melted in a matter of milliseconds and leaned against the main door.

"I guess I'm the unluckiest person in the universe!" Lily said and threw the Popsicle stick on the grass. She opened the door and entered her house.

CHAPTER FOUR

All Because Of A Tree

Green grass ruffling under my boots, I counted today's stock in my basket. Twenty-one. A good one, that was for sure.

Behind my back was a dense forest I used to cut the wood in. But I was nature-loving, so for every tree I cut, I would plant a sapling in the forest somewhere. I was strolling down the mountain.

I was doing the math of how much I would make when I ran into a big brown object.

"Ow!" I trembled and my basket fell out of my hand and onto the ground.

There it was, the same pine tree I constantly refused to cut down. In my three years of woodcutting, I had gotten somewhat attached to this tree, always seeing it on my way back to town. It grew bigger and taller as the days went by, from two metres to three and then almost thrice my height.

I patted the tree and looked at it. It really was very big. I picked up my basket, put the few planks which had fallen out and started my way back.

It was right when I passed beside it that I noticed the crack.

My eyes fell on a ginormous crack on the tree's trunk. Because of it, the tree was leaning like the Leaning Tower of Pisa.

I had never thought I would get so attached to a tree. I felt a tear escape my eye. I immediately wiped it with my wrist and contemplated all the possibilities.

A crack in a tree was very, very dangerous. According to my calculations, with the tree leaning so sloppily, the crack would only widen and the tree would cut, roll down the mountains and probably squash a dozen people to death.

"Don't worry, Piney," I reassured my tree friend. The nickname "Piney" just popped into my head. "I'll treat ya."

I put the basket away on a boulder and examined the tree.

What would I even be able to do? A crack in a tree—just thinking about fixing it was a senseless thought...

Despair is never the answer, said a voice in my head. That's something I had taught myself over time.

So I sat near the tree, staring, with a frustrated scowl on my face, at the crack in the trunk.

Then my gaze fell on my basket of wood planks I had cut and carved myself.

Could it...?

I came back to sit face-to-face with the crack with my basket on my lap. The crack was horizontal V-shaped, facing the mountainside and over the town.

I carefully cut a plank in half with my mini-saw and positioned it in the crack so that it covered the opening of the V. It stuck there, though shaking a little, it was placed fittingly.

It was a silly idea, covering a tree crack with wooden planks but it was the best idea I had.

I cut more of the planks and now the entire crack of the tree was filled with light-color wood.

I was about to go back down the mountain when I heard a creak!

Then another creak and a very ominous grrrr!

I looked back and—my basket flew out of my hand and a series of small, familiar, pieces of wood slid down to my feet. Many creaks! creaked.

I looked above and it was my worst nightmare. The crack had widened—scary and horrible enough—and the tree was gradually leaning lower, ready to be cut down.

I cursed whoever or whatever had made that crack and ran for it, as fast as possible and with as much effort as I could give it, I pushed the tree back with my hands and head, wishing someone could come and help.

The weight of the tree must have been heavier than the entire mountain itself, because my entire body felt numb, my legs slipping down the grass, a branch brushing my hair and leaves falling down.

When I heard the POOM! I was pretty sure both of us were done for—me and the tree.

A loud howl and a THUD! were enough for me to let go of the terrific weight and fall to the ground.

In what I guess were several minutes, I felt a furry paw on my forehead. Then a grunt and chirps. Then cooes, caws, puffs and possibly every animal sound imaginable.

My eyes fluttered open. I felt very nauseous, feeling dizzy and wanting to vomit all over the place. Rubbing my eyes, I stretched my body and tried to regain my vision. It was still daylight, but I felt sleepy.

All this happened because of one tree. How silly of me! I said to myself in my head.

There was a rumble in the ground. And as if like a jump-scare, a pig popped out of nowhere and appeared beside me.

"Hey!" I whimpered and slid a little away from it.

To my left was a herd of tiger cubs. I had encountered some of them in my wood quests, but God, there were so many. Must have been dozens.

A little ladybug flew and landed on my chest. I did nothing. I was too tired to even move a finger. Even blinking consumed all of my energy. So I just helplessly whistled in front of it. The little bug did some sort of backflip and flew away.

At this point, I knew I was in a dream. Or a nightmare.

A baby tiger walked near me. It purred like a domestic cat, put its paw on my chest and tilted its head as if curious to know what I was.

It put its head on my chest. I wasn't an animal expert, but I knew if a tiger puts its paw and head on your chest, you can be sure it doesn't want to murder you.

So I just stared at it, wistful to go out of this dream and see whether I would land in heaven, hell or the town hospital.

The group of baby cubs cheered, not in a human type of way, but just roared in celebration, though I had no idea what they were celebrating.

The cub which had put its head on my chest put its head away and turned its face to somewhere to my right. I turned my head to see what the cub had seen, but just saw the pig snorting.

Then, as my vision's vagueness faded, I saw a blissful sight. The pine tree, Piney, was standing still with no cracks in it, but just a bird nest on a branch and sparrows chirping on its leaves.

When I shook my head, I was able to make out where I was. I was on the same mountain, just lying a few metres away from the tree instead of lying right before it.

Only one word escaped my lips. I turned to the tiger cubs. "H-how...?"

They all purred sweetly and gently, and ran away into the forest behind them. But one cub stayed, its head still on my chest.

The cub put its gaze on my right again and I noticed it was staring at the pig. I turned to them, too, and realized there wasn't just one pig. Half a dozen pigs were snorting, playing in the grass, very much not dirty from mud. Then I saw a hole near them and noticed a large portion of the mud was gone from the ground. Then I noticed the tree...

The crack was filled in with the mud! The tigers and the pigs had united and worked on saving the tree!

"Really?" I asked the cub. It just hummed approvingly.

I lay there on the ground, doing nothing but staring at the tiger cub before me.

At last, my only thought was:

Pigs can be useful.

Laughing At The Face Of Death

The best thing that happened this week was meeting and having fun with Death.

I was sipping my cup of milkshake, sitting, leaning against the wall, on my deathbed at the pathetically young age of 21. Cancer sucks, man, I thought for the 76th time this day.

A creature entered the room, slowly opening the door, and sat on a stool near me after politely closing it. It wore a long, loose, pure black robe, with a drooping hood covering his head and a sharp, iron scythe strapped to his golden belt.

"Young man," it muttered. "Pleased to meet you."

I put my cup down on my lap with a shaky hand. "So," I said, "nice to meet you, too."

The creature got straight to the point. "We've met."

I sighed. "Yes, we have." I closed my eyes, fearful to say it again. "You've come to take me, Death."

I could almost see the lenient smile on his covered deadly face. "You are cleverer than most."

"Why would I not?" I asked, a hint of impatience in my voice. "I know what your job is. You have only failed once," I murmured, "by me."

Death straightened his face, and his hood fell back down, revealing his face. It was a skull. That's it. No flesh, no blood, no insides. Just a big bone found inside everyone.

"You knew you will fail, but still you came," I said.

"Every being shall have to face Death at least four times." Death's voice sounds like the atmosphere of a graveyard—hopeless, tragic, loss of many, yet transquil and undisturbed. Everything he says sounds like a lullaby to sing to you to your demise. "I do what I should dutifully. Parts of me are all around the world, reaping the souls of a plethora of creatures."

The side of my lips twitched. "You can't take me. It's just an encounter. Everyone faces you. Nobody says it aloud. It's an unwritten rule of life. It's like one of the terms and conditions before birth—you face him, never tell anyone."

Death quietly clapped a few times. Clap, clap, clap. "I couldn't have put it better. You're the smartest client I have had."

I nodded. "How about Albert Einstein? Leonardo da Vinci? Isaac Newton?"

Death put his hands on the side of my hospital bed. "I prefer not talking about my other clients with another. Manners, you see."

"I am pleased to meet you, Death. However, I don't feel like dying." I turned my face to the window opposing Death. "I have a lot more to accomplish before I fade out of my world."

"I have said it to you, but I shall say it again. It is not unlikely of me to go empty-handed after a meeting with an afflicted person."

"I don't wanna play no games," I said swiftly. "What do you mean? Is it my time to go, or is it not?"

"We shall find out sooner than later." Death stood up and took his scythe out.

I knitted my eyebrows, knowing what was about to happen.

But Death surprised me. Death surprises everyone. It is a thrilling, yet formidable concept.

Death surprised me greatly. He just rubbed the handle of his scythe and strapped it to his belt again.

I let out a breath I didn't know I was holding.

Death looked at me, then at the heart monitor, then beyond the window, in the sky; then back at me again. He put his bony hand on my forehead and patted me like I was his pet.

"Life awaits you," he said aloud. "It is not fitting for you to perish right now."

"Or fair," I added.

Death shook his head. "Death isn't fair. But it is fitting." He tilted his head to one side, studying my face, leading to my cup of milkshake. "I prefer a shake with cool icing on the top over a topless one. Next time we meet, I will be delighted to get that." He smiled strangely. Smiling is a weird thing. It can make anyone look beautiful. Even a smile on Death's face itself, he looked good.

Then he slowly trotted over to the exit door. I laughed. He joined in. Our amusement lasted for only some seconds, but it felt like hours.

"We shall meet again," Death said, exiting. Then he peeped in again, winked and said quietly, "Some foamy creamy shake for me next time, please," and shut the door.

I smiled, knowing I hadn't gotten out of death, but Death had just spared me. Again.

But one thing was sure. The bed I was sitting on would not be my deathbed, now.

"We shall meet again," I whispered to myself.

I turned to my nightstand and rang the bell. A worker came immediately.

"What can I do?" she asked.

"Not much." I gestured to my cup of milkshake. "I only think some cold icing on my drink would be nice. And a refill with chocolate milkshake."

CHAPTER SIX

Love And Hate

Love was an adorable creature. It was not an animal that would walk on two feet or had claws.

It was just a ball, the size of a basketball, very fluffy and furry. It had white-and-pink striped all over its skin. It would always smile and its eyes radiated happiness. It would make these cute sounds like a cat giggling.

Love also had a power called Hope that it had an unlimited source of from its mouth. If someone who was hopeless in life was walking down and Love saw them, Love would spit Hope from its mouth on them which would feel like a breeze full of confidence.

Love also had the power to blossom any plant or tree and to throw water to any thirsty creature passing by it.

Love would often whisper encouraging words to whoever picked it up like, "I love you!", "I'm Love! Please never give up!", "Choo-choo! Believe in yooou!", "You're worth it and treat yourself!", "Take breaks, buddy!", "You're beautiful as... I lost words. Nothing is as beautiful as you!" and many lines like these. Anybody who knew Love appreciated Love's work.

But somebody followed Love who Love never knew about...

Its name was Hate. Hate was always hyperactive and hated everything. It always frowned seeing people laugh with Love.

Hate was a creature that looked like a handkerchief. It always was on flames, but it did not care. It had two horns on almost every every piece of cloth of its body. It flew around discouraging people and saying things the opposite of what Love said.

Hate could summon fire anywhere and make the wind and air go in any direction he wanted.

He ususally said things like, "Hey, you, yeah you, you're a disappointment!", "I h~aaaa~te you!", "Duh, give up!", "You're gonna be a failure, haha!", "Why are you even trying!" and the worst of all: "I wish you lose weight so that there will be less of you!"

Hate also could spit something. The opposite of Hope. Despair. Hopelessness. It spat Despair on its enemies to make them even more miserable.

Love and Hate were both immune to physical pain.

One evening, Love saw Hate bullying a high schooler. She was crying as Hate glided around her, spitting Despair from his mouth.

The high schooler cried, "Please, stop it!"

"Hehe!" Hate said as he heard her sob miserably.

Love was expressionless. Love went up to her and shouted in its childish voice, "Hey! I love you!"

"You tryna take my spot, huh?" Hate said angrily.

"No, I'm not! I wanna make this girl happy!" Love said joyfully.

Hate flew away from the girl.

"Hey! Don't listen to it! You're an awesome person!" Love said, grinning as a smile appeared on the girl's face, "Now run away from here before he attacks you again, cutie!"

The girl said a hurried "Thanks so much!" and sprinted away down the streets.

"She was my victim!" Hate yelled angrily.

"Why do you do this?" Love asked, "I've never seen you!"

"You're Love. And I'm Hate."

"Oh! Now I understand! Why? Why do you do this bad stuff?"

"Because that's my job, Lovely!"

"Mmm... But that'a very bad job, Hateful."

"We can fight and see who's better."

"I don't like fights! I like peace in the world! That is my job!"

"C'mon, don't escape, Lovely!"

"Well, then, Hateful!"

"Fist fight!"

"Neither of us has fists. Just a regular fight, all right?"

Love and Hate looked at each other.

"First, we gotta go there," Hate said, gliding to a small corner.

"Why?"

"To hide this fight from the mortal human beings, Lovely."

"You know, you're evil but you're still smart, Hateful," Love complimented. Love waited for a thanks but it didn't come.

"You thinking I gonna 'return the compliment'?, Lovely?"

Love sighed and shook its head, disappointed.

"GO!" yelled Hate and it went on a quick attack on Love.

But Love dodged it. It knew if Hate was a feeling just like Love, it would not feel any physical pain. But Love could avoid attacks and defend itself.

"I know you immune to this, Lovely!" Hate yelled as Love summoned a pine tree in front him. A small pinecone dropped on Hate.

"Oops," Love said and it started to spit Hope on Hate.

"Hey!" Hate exclaimed and it started throwing Despair. Hate summoned a fire between it and Love.

"That is better!" Hate shouted and ran behind Love as Love grew tall grass around them.

"You ain't winning this, Hateful!" Love shouted hopefully.

"I'm gonna burn these green plants and red will rule!" Hate said and spat a tiny amount of Despair and flew on the pine tree.

Love puffed up. "Oof!" Love called and climbed up the tree and summoned grapfruits on every one of its branches. A group of grapefruits surrounded Hate a few metres away from Love.

"Scared, Hateful?" Love called slyly.

"Wait for my special attack, Lovely!" Hate answered and made the breeze go to Love's direction.

"Two powers? Cute!" Love was blown by a range of air.

Love had to use its secondary power. It made a water hole below the tree. Hate summoned fire on the tree's trunk.

Love summoned water on the fire and extinguished it "Pollution is bad, Hateful!"

"I'm coming, Lovely!" Hate said as it landed in the water. It glided to Love.

"You're trying but you will never get on my level, Lovely!" It said and summoned a ring of fire around itself and Love. It wrapped Love around its body.

"What now?" Hate said as it tried to suffocate Love.

"Hateful! I'm Love and I love everyone. But I never thought I would hate someone. And that only person who I feel resentment for is YOU!" Love shouted, for the first time in anger.

With Love's speech, Hate was affected toughly. For the first time, it had felt Hate: The only thing it showered on passersby in glee, it had felt it now.

Hate pulled himself away, scowling at Love.

Love breathed and summoned water on the fire ring surrounding them.

Love said something Hate had least expected. "One last move," Love said determinedly, smirking.

"Last one, Lovely," Hate said, getting a smirk on his face, too.

"Ready, Hateful?"

"I always was," Hate said.

Hate waited for Love to make a move but Love did not. While Love also waited for Hate to make a tough move, but Hate did not.

"Scared?" asked Hate.

Love smiled delightfully and shook its head.

Hate sighed, "Good."

"–for you," Love completed.

"–and you," Hate concluded.

Love made water fall on Hate and ran to the streets, but Hate pushed it hard by the wind's energy and Love was swept away very far away from Hate.

"That rubbish, Lovely." Hate smirked thinking about Love. "Still unique," It added and went back to its work: Giving Hate.

Thousands of miles away, Love whispered to itself, "Hate is a weirdo... But I gotta admit, it's got style and it's unique." Love grinned and went back to its work: Giving Love.

CHAPTER SEVEN

Sleepless Nights

"You have to do it Samira." She told herself standing before the mirror again like every morning. She put on the brightest smile wearing her school uniform, taking a final glance at herself she walked out of her room. She joined her family for the breakfast on one of the plastic chairs placed around a small table. Her father was sitting across the table reading newspaper, she cleared her throat before saying but got interrupted by her elder sister.

"I changed my subject." Her sister stated, Her father dropped the newspaper in shock, his eyes wide open. Samira sat there dumbfounded looking at her father who was disappointed by this act. "I'm sorry papa, but I couldn't do it. So I changed it yesterday." She said again.

"Do what you please, have you girls ever listened to me?" Her father said in a disappointed tone rubbing his temples hard. "All I wanted was to secure your future, what will you do after that? Work as an employee in a bank like me? I worked hard to give all three of you everything. Jiya took commerce too and now what is she doing?" He pointed at his eldest daughter who was in the kitchen helping her mother. "Now you also did what you wanted apparently she will do the same after all you're twins." He pointed at Samira who curled her fingers into a fist stopping herself from crying. Mitali just rolled her eyes and left avoiding any further arguments.

Samira picked her bag and left too muttering something about getting late. She kept thinking about something all the way to school, the school she always dreamed of but didn't feel happy at all.

"Hey, earth to Samira. What are you thinking?" Her friend asked as she was sitting all by herself like a statue. She was the only friend Samira had in the whole class or say in the whole school. Being an introvert she always struggled to open up and socialize.

"Oh. Nothing, just didn't sleep well." She said taking out her notebook. The notebook that was filled with some random words and scribbles all over.

"I've your test papers from last week. Monitor distribute it according to the names." The teacher handed the test papers to the monitor. One by one the monitor called out the names and passed the papers. He chuckled a little when a certain name displayed and made his way towards the last row.

"Samira." He handed her the paper and left giggling to himself. Samira looked at her paper with a blank expression getting an idea of why the monitor giggled. A tear came rolling down at her cheek looking at the score she got.

" 3 out of 10." She mumbled to herself and wiped her tears before anyone could notice. She flashed a smile to her friend who was sitting a row ahead of her and went back to jot everything down as the class started.

"Samira, can I have a word with you?" The teacher asked her after the class dismissed and called her in the staffroom. Fortunately no one was around the staffroom and she would be less embarrassed she thought to herself. "The reason I called you here is to ask you something." She paused to look at her and continued. " Your scores are constantly dropping down and I'm worried for you. I want to help you, if there's anything I could help you with the academics. Just ask okay." Samira nodded stood there silently with her head hung low. " You can go now. But I'll wait for you to come up." Samira whispered a quick thank you and left.

"Why did she call you?" Her friend asked when she came back to grab her bag. Samira shook her head to imply that it wasn't that important and smiled.

"Let's go get some ice cream." Samira said.

They made a beeline towards the canteen to buy some ice cream before going home. They talked a bit about random stuffs until the ice cream melted and they had to lick their fingers clean.

X

"How was school?" Her mother asked setting a plate for her. Mitali was nowhere around means she hasn't returned yet and Jiya kept her locked inside the room since breakfast and her father left for work. Samira let out a tired sigh and began eating.

" It was good." Her mother hummed in response.

She went upstairs after lunch to rest a bit when she saw Jiya sobbing. She sat beside her on the edge of the bed and stroked her back gently. Jiya looked at her and cried on her shoulders.

" Why can't he see that I'm trying. I'm trying to find a job, it's not easy but I'm trying. He always relies on you, we are not smarter than you. You've always been good with the academics. It's easy for you to be a doctor, I don't want to be a doctor. Why can't he acknowledge me for once." Jiya let out her anger and frustration through crying. She sobbed until she fell asleep. Tucking her to bed Samira went to the bathroom.

"If only she knew I'm not that smart." She mumbled to her reflection on the mirror. She washed her face and came out to find Mitali smiling ear to ear. "You look so happy." She said.

"Yeah I'm relieved that I changed the subject, being a doctor was not my thing." Mitali said and plopped down on the bed leaving a loud sigh.

Samira spent the entire evening learning formulas and diagrams for the upcoming test. But she kept forgetting everything after a while and had to start all over again. She lost the track of time , only noticed when her father came back from the office. They shared dinner together like any other day but no one uttered a word. Everyone went to their respective rooms after the dinner. Samira went upstairs to the bedroom she shared with her sisters.

Jiya and Mitali dozed off as soon as they took a step inside the room. Samira on the other hand plopped down on her chair and took out her notebook. The notebook she always kept with herself and didn't tell anyone about it. Basically it was a diary in disguise. Diaries in middle class Indian families are not something you can keep hidden.

And like any other nights she poured out her feelings into the paper that she couldn't tell anyone. She didn't know how much she could hold it inside her tiny little brain but what she did know was she's never going to tell anyone.

" I failed again, it took me a whole month to muster up the courage to finally tell papa that I couldn't do this. I'm not made to be a doctor and I don't understand the theories and scientific reasons behind everything. I'm sorry that I failed in my test, even if I don't want to... I'm still trying hard.

I don't know where life would take me? Or where I'll be in next 10 years?

All I want is to gather some courage to tell everyone that I cannot do this anymore without disappointing anyone."

She closed the book and lied down on the mattress to get some sleep but little did she know there was no way she could sleep with these thoughts buzzing inside her head. The thoughts of being a coward who could not stand for herself. The thoughts that's going to keep her awake for the rest of the night. She closed her eyes in a hope to wake up with some courage to stand for herself next day.

CHAPTER EIGHT

Guess We All Know

It was finally lunchtime. I was amazed when I learned that the geography class was only an hour long. It felt like a millenia.

After gobbling down my sandwich, I asked Suzy, Paul, Dory and June to play Hide-and-Seek in the playground. We gathered at the edge of the mini forest near our school.

"So, who'll be the seeker?" June asked.

"Paul," Suzy immediately replied.

"Voting again?" Dory said. "I say Paul too."

"Benny," June said.

I voted, "Paul!"

Paul groaned, "You guys have already decided. Why do you need my vote? I say myself."

"Okay," I said. I immediately ran down the grassy lanes, knowing nobody was gonna find me, a tiny 5th grader, in a forest!

"Hey, Benny!" I heard Suzy call out, but I was too far to go back now. I found myself in a pine-trees area that has pine cones spread in all directions.

I ran into a fluffy shrub, and crawled past it.

There was a long river with big rocks near it. Tall, dark, mystic, firm, spruce trees touched the sky as the wind rustled north. Some orange parrots fluttered across the river, mimicking the other birds.

I glanced at all sides. I found a hole in a tree to my left, but it was too high. But I knew a way.

I grabbed a branch and stomped my leg against the bark. I took branches one-by-one, on each hand, and finally reached the small cubicle in the tree. I was surprised that there was no one there, so I happily hopped into it and peeped down.

"Whoa... wow," I murmured. I was even more sure that nobody was going to find me. I was more than ready to pluck some fruits and munch on them as Paul struggled to seek me.

Then I heard a humanly screech.

At first I thought it must be a parrot. Then I realised even if it was a parrot, it would need something to mimic off of, so I looked down.

I was right. Many parrots were mimicking a series of screams and shrieks. Someone was in danger and I needed to see. At once, I slung my legs down and climbed down and landed on a fortunately soft pine cone.

It still poked a little and I panicked. "Ow!" I leaped out of the way to see a shadow hovering by a bush. "Who is it?!"

June's voice shouted, "Benny! Are you okay?"

I ran up to her. Our other friends were standing behind her, whimpering and drenched in something red and wet.

"G-guys?" I said, horrified.

"You need to see this," Suzy said.

"Wh-why are you guys covered in..." I was too scared to say it, but I knew it was true. "In... blood?"

"C'mere, Ben," Dory said.

I followed them to the end of the forest and to the canteen area. Everyone had gone to the basketball court, because it was the finale today.

"Here," Paul said. We all went inside the empty canteen. We went near the smoothy refrigerator where the smoothies were stored.

Suzy opened the door. I screamed

Sitting there, with its knee to its nose and its hands around its folded legs, was a dead body wearing a loose pink cloak, and with long brown hair. A small pipe lay glued to its side, splattering red liquid everywhere.

"Wh-who is this?" I asked. "This isn't blood, right?"

"We don't know. We were about to go looking for you in the forest with a smoothy snack, but instead we found... whatever this is..." Suzy crossed her arms.

That day, all of us sat in the canteen and shared a pizza. None of us said a word. We silently ate the pizza and stayed there, staring at each other, as if one of us was an impostor and knew what that corpse-and-red-liquid-pumping-from-pipe-in-fridge stuff was about.

When everyone came back from the basketball match, they celebrated widely for our school's victory, but we waited for an adult.

When our art teacher came, we immediately informed him about it, and he witnessed the situation inside the smoothy refrigerator.

The next day we asked him if what we saw was even real. After he nodded a firm assent, we asked him who the corpse was and why there was red stuff coming from a pipe and if it was real blood.

His answer only gave us more questions, but it did give us a life lesson.

He said, with a hint of grief in his voice, "Some things are better kept a mystery. When all the secrets are revealed... those secrets can destroy you."

CHAPTER NINE

As If

"Dance as if no one is watching. Sing as if no one is listening. Love as if you have never been hurt."

(Mentions of Suicide)

It never occurred to me how many secrets I had been keeping from everyone, and how much I was scared of being perceived as a weak or emotional person.

Crying was never the option. Whenever I cried, I'd be ashamed. All in the 18 years of my life, I lied.

I lied to parents that I liked their company, and to my friends that I was fine, and to my relatives that I was doing well, and to the kind man I met at the school gates every day, and even... even to my doctor that I had no problem.

When I was hurt, I would try to get nicer to my family. I would try to get better by going to watch some cute animals.

Countless nights I spent trying to think how I would definitely gobble down my meal the next day, only to drink a sip of milk and say I was not hungry.

I was often neglected, but I denied it. I just thought that my parents had other things to worry about rather than play with some baby. I didn't consider said baby was their baby. Their only child.

I remember one time I tore off a piece of ad on a newspaper which had just a yellow wallpaper. On that I wrote the darkest words ever.

I had written, I wish I could leave everyone I know. Nobody seems to care for me. I could easily live on my own. Screw all these families and friends.

The worst part? I was only 12.

The strangest thing was that I never considered suicide. I always thought of it as a meaningless act. Killing yourself would do nothing good, I would think. But I sympathized with those who had done it or were considering it.

Almost every night during my teenage years, I would quietly say, "If you are listening to me, please don't kill yourself. You are worth it." I wished that if anyone, anyone, could hear it, it would make them happy.

When I finally moved out of my parents' house, I had never felt more free.

I had also never thought how much it would mean when someone asked a single question.

The question came from my therapist: What made you want to go for therapy today?

Even though it must've been obvious, I'd thought I didn't have that bad of a past.

Only when was this inquiry uttered that I questioned everything about my childhood.

I remembered something I had read in a post on some Social Media app; Dance as if no one is watching. Sing as if no one is listening. Love as if you have never been hurt.

I'd been involuntarily following that for years. Oftentimes in my childhood, I'd say to myself, It isn't that bad! Just act as if you've never been hurt.

My heart almost leaped out of my throat.

It was this single quote that had been keeping me alive. This was why I didn't consider suicide. My mind had thought that I wasn't in the worst situation. There were people suffering way more.

I yelped. I said to myself in my mind, Cry as if you've always been hurt. Which was true.

For the first time in my life, I wasn't ashamed to cry

CHAPTER TEN

In The Cage

The night was darker and terrifying and no possible way to run along. The sound coming from the impact of the wind with the tall trees sent shivers down the spine. No roads and civilisation so far. You were running, running deep into the woods with no source of light. Your feet felt numb from constant running. But why were you running? You ran as fast as you could looking behind all the time like someone was chasing you. Were you running from someone?

After running from a while you saw a little light coming from a small cottage. You took a deep breath and like some fire ignited inside your body you ran with your full speed to approach the light.

Finally you reached a cottage from where the light was glowing. The fence was broken, slowly slowly with quiet and small steps you reached for the door. You peeked behind last time before knocking at the door.

"Is anybody-" the door unlocked on it's own.

You quietly went inside and closed the door.

The house was well illuminated and warm but nobody was around. The dinner was served at the table beside the fireplace. Just like someone was waiting for a company. Many photographs and painting were nailed at the walls of the room.

"Isn't it pretty." A voice came from behind. You flinched at the voice. An old woman was coming out from the kitchen with a dessert on her hands.

"My son loves to paint." She approached you.

You were terrified yet confused for how calm she looked by your presence.

"Oh, girl you look dirty. Why don't you freshen up." She pushed you towards the bathroom with a pair of clean clothes and towel.

You were quick to respond with a no. You were confused with her behaviour. Why she was helping an intruder? Why? These thoughts were telling you to refuse her offer.

But you stood there still. You were afraid to go out and encounter the person who was chasing you.

"You are scared of me? I see. Anyone would be...huh.... I don't get visits. Others think of me as an old crazy woman who lives in the forest and scares people." You were just staring at her, so afraid to take a step either way.

"You must be thinking I'm crazy. Well what a poor old lady can afford? I had a son who lives in the city to make some money but suddenly 3 years ago he stopped visiting. Police told me my son got missing. I have been waiting since then everyday with his favourite food.... crazy...isn't it? The police declared him dead but I don't believe them. You can go back if you want. It's dark out here . I would have preferred to stay." She finished.

Slowly you took a step towards her. You were afraid to go out and face that man again and somehow the old lady seem trustable. She convinced you that she meant no harm. She convinced you to stay. You changed into comfortable clothes and took a seat on through dining.

It was indeed a nice meal that you had in past few days you thought. But there was something eerie about the strange peace around the house despite of the fact that the woman kept talking to you for which you just nodded in response. But she didn't force you for talking like she sensed the fear inside you and how scared you were.

"Here take some tea." She offered you tea after dinner.

You just nodded. She went straight to the drawer placed in the living room to find something. After ruffling through the stuffs she took out a photo album. The cover was torn out and pages were a little dirty with an old smell of books.She placed the album on your lap and started to tell some more stories about her son.

"That's him, my son....." She pointed at the man on the photo with a sickle on his hand.

Somehow that man seemed familiar to you but your memories were fading slowly followed by drowsiness that you were feeling. Was it because you were tired? Or maybe you didn't sleep properly past days? Or is it the tea? You thought.

Quickly you snapped out from your thoughts and took a closer look at the picture. You knew him....you knew that face.....you knew that face behind you.....you remembered the man who was chasing you.....yes, the boy from the picture was the one who was chasing you in the woods.

Suddenly you felt dizzy and your visions became blurry. You saw the woman sitting in front of you. She was smiling and the last thing that you remember is she whispered something in your ear. "Thank you." And you passed out.

Next morning there was a loud banging on the door. It became louder but no one was answering. You heard the door but couldn't make it to the door. After a while the door broke open and 5 men in uniform came inside calling for you. But for some reason you couldn't respond. But why?

"Mam are you okey?" One of them helped the woman to stand up.

But who was she....she wasn't here last night as you remember. But why she looked familiar? She wore the same clothes that you wore before changing. Who was she? And where was the old woman? You thought.

"Mam, let's get you out of here." The inspector helped the lady to get up. She looked terrified unable to figure out what happened and how she ended up in that house.

I called for help but for some reason my voice was inaudible for them. I tried to reach out to them but something was stopping me to move forward like an invisible wall.

I saw her standing up slowly from the couch where she was laying earlier. She had long hair that was messed up just like me. She wore same clothes that I remember I was wearing last night. She was going out with the policemen she turned around just before stepping outside. An evil grin on her face and she looked directly at me. Now I remember the woman was me.

How is this possible? Why they couldn't see you? Where were you? These thoughts were running through your mind. You were getting furious by each second that passed. You were screaming your lungs out but it went unnoticed.

Slowly the door closed and the woman left with them. The sound made from the friction between tires and the grass was getting farther. The place became darker and there was nowhere you could go....no one to help you.....just you in the dark....you were caged.